A NOTE TO PARENTS

When your children are ready to "step into reading," giving them the right books is as crucial as giving them the right food to eat. **Step into Reading Books** present exciting stories and information reinforced with lively, colorful illustrations that make learning to read fun, satisfying, and worthwhile. They are priced so that acquiring an entire library of them is affordable. And they are beginning readers with a difference—they're written on five levels.

Early Step into Reading Books are designed for brand-new readers, with large type and only one or two lines of very simple text per page. **Step 1 Books** feature the same easy-to-read type as the Early Step into Reading Books, but with more words per page. **Step 2 Books** are both longer and slightly more difficult, while **Step 3 Books** introduce readers to paragraphs and fully developed plot lines. **Step 4 Books** offer exciting nonfiction for the increasingly independent reader.

The grade levels assigned to the five steps—preschool through kindergarten for the Early Books, preschool through grade 1 for Step 1, grades 1 through 3 for Step 2, grades 2 through 3 for Step 3, and grades 2 through 4 for Step 4—are intended only as guides. Some children move through all five steps very rapidly; others climb the steps over a period of several years. Either way, these books will help your child "step into reading" in style!

Random House 🏠 New York

Text copyright © 1997 by Marilyn Sadler. Illustrations copyright © 1997 by Roger Bollen.
All rights reserved under International and Pan-American Copyright Conventions.
Published in the United States by Random House, Inc., New York, and simultaneously
in Canada by Random House of Canada Limited, Toronto.

http://www.randomhouse.com/

Library of Congress Cataloging-in-Publication Data
Sadler, Marilyn. The parakeet girl / by Marilyn Sadler ; illustrated by Roger Bollen.
p. cm. — (Step into reading. A step 2 book)
SUMMARY: Emma tries several pets before she becomes best friends with her parakeet Henry,
but she finds that friendship threatened when her brother Bruce buys another parakeet.
ISBN 0-679-87289-2 (pbk.) — ISBN 0-679-97289-7 (lib. bdg.)
[1. Parakeets—Fiction. 2. Pets—Fiction. 3. Friendship—Fiction.] I. Bollen, Roger, ill.
II. Title. III. Series: Step into reading. Step 2 book.
PZ7.S1239Par 1997 [E]—dc20 95-9646
Printed in the United States of America 10 9 8 7 6 5 4
STEP INTO READING is a registered trademark of Random House, Inc.

Step into Reading®

The PARAKEET GIRL

by Marilyn Sadler

illustrated by Roger Bollen

A Step 2 Book

Emma Tuttle wanted a pet

of her very own

more than anything else

in the world.

So on her sixth birthday,

Emma's parents gave her a puppy.

Emma loved her puppy.

She gave him the best life

a puppy could have.

She fed him three times a day…

…no matter how funny

his food smelled.

She took him for walks…

…no matter how cold it was.

She threw his ball for him…

…no matter how many times

he brought it back.

But it did not matter

what Emma did.

Her puppy liked her mother better.

"He's Mom's dog,"

said her brother, Bruce.

So one day, Emma

came home with a kitten.

"He was free!"

she told her mother.

Emma loved her kitten,

and her kitten loved her.

He followed her everywhere.

He rubbed up against her legs.

He even sat on her lap

and let her pet him.

There was just one problem...

...he made her sneeze.

So Emma bought a goldfish.

But he was not the right pet either.

He did not come when she called him.

He did not like to be petted.

And, worst of all,

he never seemed happy to see her.

Emma took her goldfish

back to the pet store.

"I guess there's no pet for me,"

she said sadly.

Then, to Emma's surprise,

a parakeet landed on top of her head.

"Pretty bird, pretty bird,"

said the parakeet.

Emma liked the idea

of a pet that could talk.

She bought the parakeet

and named him Henry.

Emma took Henry home.

"He can talk!"

she told her parents.

"Pretty bird, pretty bird,"

said Henry.

He did not know how

to say anything else.

That night,

Emma decided to teach Henry

every word in the dictionary.

She read them all, from A to Z.

Then she waited

to hear what Henry could say.

Henry opened his beak.

"Aardvark," he said.

When Emma woke up

the next morning,

Henry was on her bedpost.

She was so happy to see him.

He was so happy to see her.

Henry was the perfect pet.

Soon Emma and Henry

became best friends.

They did everything together.

Emma took Henry with her

to her piano lessons.

She took Henry with her

to the dentist.

She even took Henry with her
when she had her picture taken.
Emma just didn't look right anymore
without Henry on top of her head.

One morning, Emma decided
to take Henry to school.

But Emma's teacher

was not happy to see him.

"You know the rules,"

said Mrs. Crump.

"No birds, bugs, frogs, or snakes."

"I'm sorry," said Emma.

She had forgotten

that Henry was a bird.

Emma's class was learning
all about Africa that day.
"Which animal lives in Africa
and has a long snout?"
asked Mrs. Crump.
"Aardvark," said Henry.
After that, Henry
could come to school
whenever he wanted.

Henry was a big help to Mrs. Crump.

He collected homework.

He picked up litter.

He sharpened pencils.

Mrs. Crump loved Henry.

So did Emma's friends.

"Can he sit on my head today?"

"It's my turn!"

"No, it's MY turn!"

Before long,

Emma became known as

The Parakeet Girl.

Then, one day,

Bruce asked if he could take

Henry to school with him.

"I'll bring him right home

afterward," he said.

But Emma didn't want

to let Henry out of her sight.

"Sorry," said Emma.

Emma and Henry were surprised
when they got home from school.
Bruce had bought
his own parakeet.
"Her name is Kate," said Bruce.
"Pretty bird!" said Henry.

When Emma got ready

for bed that night,

Henry was not on her head.

She searched everywhere for him.

At last she went into Bruce's room.

There was Henry,

sitting beside Kate's cage.

"Aardvark," said Henry.

"Aardvark," said Kate.

Emma took Henry

and put him in his cage.

She was so upset,

she even put on his cover.

Emma went to bed.

But she could not sleep.

Henry would not stop

talking about Kate.

"Pretty bird, pretty bird,

pretty bird, pretty bird,

pretty bird, pretty bird,

pretty bird, pretty bird!" he cried.

Four hundred and fifty-two times.

The next day,

Henry did not want

to go to school.

Emma tried to reason with him.

But Henry would not listen.

She had to take him to school

in his cage.

When they got to school,

Emma set Henry free.

He flew to the window.

"PRETTY BIRRRRRRRRRRRRRD!"

he shouted.

Henry refused to collect homework.

He chewed the erasers off pencils.

He even dive-bombed Mrs. Crump.

Mrs. Crump had no choice
but to send him home.

That night,

Emma was as sad as could be.

"Henry likes Kate better than me!"

she cried.

Then she looked into Henry's eyes.

She saw the saddest face

she had ever seen.

It was even sadder than hers.

So Emma did the only thing
she could do.

She set Henry free.

He flew right to Kate.

After that, Emma was not herself.

One day, she even took

Henry's empty cage to school.

Emma's parents tried
to make Emma happy.
They offered to buy her
another parakeet.
But Emma was not interested.

Then, one morning,

Emma thought she heard

something unusual.

It sounded like Henry.

But it also sounded like Kate.

Emma ran into Bruce's room.

She couldn't believe her eyes.

Henry and Kate had two babies!

They were the prettiest parakeets

Emma had ever seen!

"Pretty babies, pretty babies,"

whispered Emma.

Emma took good care

of the babies.

She fed them.

She cleaned their cage.

She read them every word

in the dictionary.

44

Emma even took

the parakeet babies to school.

Mrs. Crump was glad to see them—

her pencils needed sharpening.

From then on,

Emma was as happy as could be.

She had wanted a pet

of her very own

more than anything else

in the world.

Now she had *two*...

...Henry Jr. and Henrietta.